Peter Pan

The Young Collector's
Illustrated Classics

Peter Pan

By
J.M. Barrie

Adapted by
D.J. Arneson

Illustrated by
Eva Clift

Contents

Chapter

Peter Breaks Through

One day when she was a very little girl, Wendy picked a flower from the garden to show her mother. Mrs. Darling held the flower over her heart. "Oh, Wendy," she said with a loving smile, "why can't you stay like this forever!" Wendy was just two years old, but from that moment on she knew that all children, except one, must grow up.

Wendy's mother was a lovely lady. Mr. Darling knew that when he married her. He loved her and she loved him. He liked to boast that she also respected him, which she did.

At first the Darlings worried if they

could afford children. But before each child was born, Mrs. Darling said, "Of course we can, George. We'll watch every penny." First came Wendy, then John, and Michael was last. 134

The Darlings had a nurse for the children because Mrs. Darling liked everything just so, and Mr. Darling wanted to be just like their neighbors. But since they were poor, the nurse was Nana, a very proper Newfoundland dog they found in Kensington Gardens.

Nana was a very good nurse. She learned to be a nurse by watching the other nurses in the park. She made sure the children bathed properly. She knew when a cough was just a cough and nothing serious. And if one of them cried at night, she was up in an instant to see why. That was easy because she lived in the children's room.

When the children started school, Nana made sure they got there safely. She walked primly alongside, butting anyone who strayed back into line. She made

Peter Pan

sure John didn't forget his soccer sweater, and if it looked like rain, she carried an umbrella in her mouth. At school, Nana stayed in the basement while the children sat in classrooms upstairs.

Nana didn't like Mrs. Darling's friends to make surprise visits to the children's room, but if they came, she quickly dressed Michael in a clean outfit, brushed Wendy's hair, and tried her best to do something with John's hair. She was a very proper nurse, even though Mr. Darling wondered if the neighbors thought it odd that they had a dog for a nurse. After all, he had his position in the city to consider.

There never was a happier family until the coming of Peter Pan.

Mrs. Darling first heard of Peter while tidying up her children's minds when they were asleep. Children don't know mothers do this, but they do. It's a little like tidying up drawers. Every child has a special place called Neverland filled with strange and wonderful things that are his or her

very own. Every Neverland is different. Some have rivers and reefs and gnomes and princes and caves of every kind. Others, like John's, had a lagoon where he lived on the sand in a boat turned upside down. Michael's also had a lagoon but he lived in a wigwam, while Wendy's had a house made of leaves. Neverland is filled with wonderful adventures and at night, just before you go to sleep, it seems very, very real.

Mrs. Darling knew nobody named

Peter, but there he was in each child's mind.

"Who is Peter?" she asked Wendy.

"Why, he is Peter Pan," Wendy replied.

At first, Mrs. Darling was puzzled. Then she remembered her own childhood and someone called Peter Pan who was said to live with fairies. People said he comforted children. Mrs. Darling believed in him then, "But he is grown up now," she said to Wendy.

"Oh, no," Wendy said. "He isn't grown up at all and he's just my size."

When Mrs. Darling told Mr. Darling about Peter Pan, he laughed and said it was some of Nana's nonsense. "Forget it and it will go away," he said. But it didn't.

One morning Wendy awoke to find tree leaves scattered about the bedroom floor. They weren't there when she and the boys went to bed. "Oh, it was just Peter," she said when her mother asked how they got there. "He didn't wipe his feet as he should when he comes in the window." Wendy smiled. "Sometimes he comes in at night and plays his pipes at the foot of my bed," she said.

Mrs. Darling was shocked. "Why, you must have been dreaming," she said. But the leaves were real and came from a tree she had never seen before.

Wendy had not been dreaming and the next night an extraordinary adventure began.

It was Nana's night off and Mrs. Darling tucked the children into bed. She gazed at them tenderly as she sat by the fireplace to sew. The fire was warm and the room was bathed in soft light. Soon she began to doze. While she slept, she had a dream.

In the dream, Neverland came much too near and a strange boy got out. The boy had torn the curtain that usually covers Neverland, and Wendy and John and Michael were peeking through.

Mrs. Darling dreamed the nursery window blew open and the boy flew into the room. She thought she recognized him. At his side was a tiny bright light no bigger

than a fist. It darted through the room as if it were alive.

The strange light awakened Mrs. Darling. She put her hand to her mouth in surprise for she knew at once that the boy was Peter Pan.

Mrs. Darling screamed at the sight of the strange boy. At that moment Nana entered the room, back from her evening out. She, too, saw the boy, and not knowing what to think, leaped at him with a fierce growl.

Chapter

2

The
Shadow

Peter nimbly darted to the window with Nana snapping at his toes. He quickly leaped through the open window which closed with a bang behind him.

Mrs. Darling screamed again, for she was certain the boy was killed. After all, the children's room was three stories from the street. She ran to the window to see where he had fallen, but the street was clear. Mrs. Darling looked into the dark night sky. It was empty except for a bright shooting star.

Nana stood by the window clutching something in her mouth. It was the boy's shadow. The closing window had torn it

off as neatly as a sheet of paper from a roll. It was an ordinary shadow and Nana knew immediately what to do. She hung it out the window so the boy could find it without disturbing the children.

"We can't leave it there," Mrs. Darling said. "It will look like wash hung out to dry. What would the neighbors think?" She thought to show the shadow to Mr. Darling, but he would only say, "That's what happens when you have a dog for a nurse." Since she had to do something,

Mrs. Darling rolled up the shadow and tucked it away in a drawer. She would leave it there until the right time came to tell her husband what had happened.

The right time came the very next Friday. It was a day the Darlings would never, ever forget.

"I should have known to be more careful on a Friday," Mrs. Darling said later.

Mr. Darling patted her tenderly on the shoulder. "No, my dear," he said, "I am responsible for what happened."

"No. It was my fault," Mrs. Darling replied.

They could not agree on who was to blame, nor could they forget the events of that fateful day.

"If only I had not accepted the invitation to dine at our neighbors," Mrs. Darling said.

"If only I had not poured my medicine into Nana's bowl," Mr. Darling said.

Nana's eyes clouded up as if to say, "If only I had pretended to like the medicine." Mr. Darling wiped away Nana's tears.

Each one felt they alone were to blame. But Mrs. Darling never blamed Peter.

And so they sat in the empty nursery night after night, remembering the events of that dreadful Friday evening.

It had started quite ordinarily. Nana filled Michael's bath and carried him to it on her broad back. "I won't go to bed," Michael said as if he made the rules, "I won't, I won't."

Mrs. Darling entered the nursery wearing a lovely evening gown. Around her neck was the necklace Mr. Darling gave her and on her wrist was Wendy's bracelet, which she borrowed. Wendy loved to see her dressed so prettily.

Wendy and John were pretending to be Mr. and Mrs. Darling. First John said, "Mrs. Darling, you have a baby daughter." Hearing that, Wendy danced for joy, just as her mother must have when she was born. Then John said, "And now you have a baby son," meaning himself when he was born. Wendy smiled brightly at the news.

"I want to be born, too," Michael said as he came from his bath.

"We don't want any more children," John said.

Michael's face clouded and he nearly burst into tears. "Nobody wants me," he said.

"I do!" Wendy said.

Michael was not sure she meant it. "A boy or a girl?" he asked.

"A boy!" Wendy shouted, and Michael leaped happily into her arms.

The Darlings and Nana remembered that last night the children were in the nursery. "That was when I dashed in, wasn't it?" Mr. Darling said.

Mr. Darling was also dressing for their dinner out, but he could not tie his tie. He rushed into the nursery with an untied tie dangling from his hand.

"This tie refuses to tie around my neck," he said. "It does quite well around the bedpost, but if it will not tie around my neck, we will not go to dinner. If we don't go to dinner, I won't ever go to my

office again. If I don't go to the office, we shall starve and our children will be thrown into the street."

Mrs. Darling was calm. "Let me do it, dear," she said, because she knew that's exactly what he'd come for. The children gathered around to learn if they would be thrown into the street or not. With quick hands, Mrs. Darling tied the rebellious tie. Once it was done, Mr. Darling relaxed. Soon the whole family was dancing gaily around the room.

"What fun it was," Mrs. Darling said, recalling that Friday night.

"Our last romp together," Mr. Darling said with a sigh.

Mrs. Darling's face turned sad. "They were ours, and now they are gone," she said. But even the sadness could not stop the Darlings' memories of that night.

Nana had joined the happy throng. As she romped amid the flying feet she brushed against Mr. Darling's brand-new trousers, covering them with hair.

"Oh, what a mistake to have a dog for

a nurse," he said angrily.

Mrs. Darling brushed away the hairs. "She is a treasure," she said.

"I have the feeling she thinks the children are puppies," Mr. Darling said.

Mrs. Darling shook her head. "No, George, I'm sure she knows they have souls."

Mr. Darling rubbed his chin. "Well, *you* may be sure," he said, "but I'm not."

To quickly change the subject, Mrs.

Darling told her husband about the strange boy who had flown in the window.

"Nonsense," Mr. Darling said.

"Then let me show you," Mrs. Darling said. She went to the drawer and pulled out the shadow.

"Hmm," Mr. Darling said, rubbing his chin once more, but this time in earnest. "It's nobody I know," he said as he examined the shadow, "but he looks like a scoundrel if you ask me."

Just then, Nana entered with a bottle of Michael's medicine in her mouth.

"I don't want to take my medicine," Michael cried.

"I'll get you some chocolate to make it easier to take," Mrs. Darling said, leaving the room.

"Don't pamper him," Mr. Darling said to his wife. He turned to Michael. "When I was your age, I took my medicine without a sound," he said to his son. "I even knew to thank my parents for giving me medicine to make me well." He believed what he was saying, and Wendy believed it, too.

"The medicine you have to take now is worse, isn't it?" Wendy asked her father.

"Much," Mr. Darling said. "Why, if I knew where it was, I'd take some to show you how easy it is."

Wendy smiled brightly. "I know where it is, Father," she said. She hurried out of the room before Mr. Darling could stop her.

Mr. Darling felt suddenly ill, but not in a way that medicine could help. He turned to John and said quietly, "My medicine is beastly stuff to take, John. It is the nasty, sticky kind."

Wendy returned with Mr. Darling's medicine in a glass. "Here it is," she said, handing him the glass.

"It will soon be over, Father," John said cheerily.

"Michael has to take his first," Mr. Darling said.

"No, you first," Michael said suspiciously.

"It will make me sick," Mr. Darling replied.

"Take it, Father," said John.

"Hold your tongue," Mr. Darling shot back.

Wendy was quite puzzled.

"I thought you said you didn't mind taking your medicine, Father," she said.

"That's not the point," Mr. Darling said. He glanced around for an excuse not to take his medicine. He spied the spoon with Michael's medicine. "The point is, I have more medicine in my glass than

Michael has in his spoon," he said proudly. "And that's not fair."

Michael was not persuaded. "I'm waiting," he said coldly.

"That's easy for you to say," Mr. Darling responded.

"Father's a cowardly custard," Michael laughed.

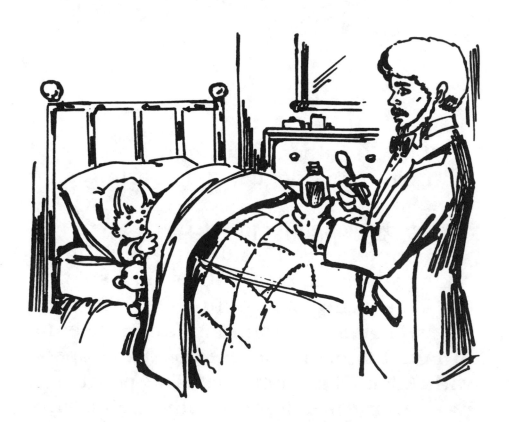

"Well, so are you," Mr. Darling said weakly.

"I'm not afraid to take my medicine," Michael said.

"Neither am I," Mr. Darling answered without thinking.

"Well, take it then," Michael said quickly.

Wendy stepped between them. "Why don't you both take your medicine at the same time?" she said. "I'll count to three." It was a splendid idea.

"All right," Mr. Darling agreed. "Are you ready, Michael?"

Michael nodded.

"One, two, three," Wendy counted.

Michael took his medicine, but Mr. Darling quickly slipped his glass behind his back.

"No fair!" Michael shouted.

"Oh, Father!" Wendy exclaimed.

Just then Nana stepped out of the room. Mr. Darling quickly changed the subject.

"I just thought of a splendid joke," he

said with a mischievous grin. "I'll put my medicine into Nana's bowl and she'll drink it and never know."

He poured the milky looking medicine into the dog's bowl before anyone could say no.

"What fun!" Mr. Darling said.

The children eyed their father with scolding looks. They said nothing when Mrs. Darling and Nana returned to the nursery.

Mr. Darling petted Nana fondly. "Good dog," he said. "Here's some milk in your bowl."

Nana wagged her fluffy tail as she quickly drank the medicine. The tail suddenly stopped wagging. She turned to Mr. Darling with a sad look. She tucked her tail between her legs and crept to her bed.

Mr. Darling was terribly ashamed of what he'd done, but he refused to admit it.

Mrs. Darling sniffed the bowl. "Oh, George," she said with reproach. "It's your medicine."

"I was only joking," Mr. Darling said.

Wendy went to Nana's side and hugged the dog.

"A lot of good it does to be funny around here," Mr. Darling said. "After all, who am I except the one who earns the money so we all can live."

He realized his argument was weak, but he had no other. He could not afford to look weak in front of his family.

"You coddle that dog, but you won't let me make a joke. So be it. I will not have that dog ruling my house for another minute."

Nana knew instantly what he was saying. The children did too and they began to cry. Mr. Darling felt strong again. "I've made my decision," he said, looking down at Nana. "The proper place for you is in the yard and that's where you are going this instant."

Mrs. Darling stepped in to put things right. "George," she said in a whisper, "remember what I told you about that boy?"

Mr. Darling did not listen. He was determined to show one and all who was the master in the family. "Come with me, Nana," he said firmly. Nana did not move, so he grabbed her collar and dragged her from the room. He was ashamed of himself, but he could not stop.

After he tied Nana in the backyard, Mr. Darling sat alone for a moment. He put his hands to his eyes and rubbed. He was very unhappy with what he had done.

In the meantime, Mrs. Darling put the children to bed. They went quietly. As Mrs. Darling lit the night-lights, the sound of distant barking entered the room.

"Nana is unhappy because Father is

chaining her in the yard," John said.

Wendy listened closely. "That's not her sad bark," she said. "That's the bark she gives when she smells danger."

Mrs. Darling shivered. "Are you sure, Wendy?" she asked nervously.

"Oh, yes!" Wendy said.

Mrs. Darling quivered. She stepped to the window and tested it. It was securely fastened. She looked into the sky. It was filled with stars that seemed to crowd around the house as if they were watching to see what would happen. Mrs. Darling put her hand to her heart. "Oh, I wish we weren't going out tonight," she cried.

Michael was already half-asleep, but he heard his mother's cry. "Can anything harm us when the night-lights are on?" he asked quietly.

"Nothing, precious," she said. "They are a mother's eyes and stay behind to guard you." She went from bed to bed singing a little song of protection over each child. Michael threw his arms around her.

"Oh, mother," he said. "I am so glad for you."

They were the last words she would hear from him for a long, long time.

Mr. and Mrs. Darling stepped out of Number 14 and carefully made their way down the street over a layer of newly fallen snow. The moment the door to their home closed, something stirred in the dark, star-filled sky.

Often, Peter liked to dart behind the stars and try to blow them out. But tonight the stars were watching the street below. They loved fun, and so, tonight, they were happy to see the grown-ups would not be home.

"Now, Peter!" the smallest star in the entire Milky Way cried out. "*Now!*"

Chapter

3

Come Away, Come Away!

Shortly after Mr. and Mrs. Darling left the house, the night-lights in the nursery went out. In their place was another, much brighter light. It flew about the room, zipping from drawer to closet as if looking for something. It came to a rest on top of a dresser. It turned out not to be a light at all, but a tiny fairy no bigger than a fist. She was dressed in an exquisite gown made from a leaf. Her name was Tinker Bell. The children did not see her because they were sound asleep.

A moment later the window flew open and Peter dropped in. "Tink?" he called. "Where are you?" He spied her inside a glass jug. "Come out of there and tell me where to find my shadow."

The sound of tiny bells filled the room. It was fairy talk and it told Peter his shadow was in the chest of drawers. Peter emptied the drawers one by one until he found his missing shadow. He was so pleased to have his shadow back, he slammed the drawer closed without looking. Tinker Bell was left inside.

Peter tried to stick his shadow to his feet but it would not stick. He wet it and rubbed it with soap, but the shadow refused to stay put. Peter sat on the floor and began to cry.

This woke Wendy. "Why are you crying, boy?" she asked.

Peter stood and bowed gracefully the way he had learned from the fairies. Wendy stood up in bed and bowed back.

"What's your name?" Peter asked.

"Wendy Moira Angela Darling," Wendy replied. "What's yours?"

"Peter Pan," Peter said.

"Where do you live?" Wendy asked.

Peter glanced out the window. "Second from the right and then straight on 'til morning," he said.

"What a funny address," Wendy said. "Is that what they write on your letters?"

Peter frowned. "I don't get letters," he said.

"Well, is that what they write on your mother's letters?" Wendy asked politely.

"I don't have a mother," Peter said quickly, "and I don't care to have one."

Wendy went to Peter's side. "No wonder you were crying," she said.

"I wasn't crying about mothers," Peter

said indignantly. "My shadow won't stay on."

"How awful," Wendy said as she examined the wrinkled shadow. "I shall sew it on."

With a needle and thread, she did just that.

The moment the shadow was attached, Peter leaped with joy. "How clever I am," he said, forgetting it was Wendy and not he who repaired his shadow.

"You are very conceited," Wendy said, "and cocky, too." She was upset.

Peter changed his tone. "Don't be upset, Wendy," he said sweetly. "You are worth 20 boys."

Wendy could not resist. "Do you really think so, Peter?" she asked.

"Yes, I do," Peter replied. He sat down on the side of the bed next to Wendy.

"Then I shall give you a kiss," Wendy said.

Peter put out his hand to receive the kiss. He did not know what a kiss was. Wendy quickly handed him a thimble so

his feelings would not be hurt. In return, Peter gave her an acorn button. She accepted it graciously.

"I shall wear it on a chain around my neck," she said. How fortunate that would be, though just now Wendy could not know why.

Wendy was very interested in Peter. "How old are you?" she asked.

Peter squirmed. "I don't know," he said. "I ran away the day I was born."

"Why did you do a thing like that?" Wendy asked.

Peter was very uncomfortable. "I heard my father and mother talking about what I should be when I grow up," he said at last. Then, looking Wendy straight in the eye, he said sharply, "I don't ever want to be grown-up. I want to stay a little boy and have fun! That's why I ran away to live with the fairies."

Wendy's fascination grew. She asked dozens of questions about fairies. They seemed quite marvelous because her own life was so home-like. Peter was surprised because fairies were a nuisance to him, even though he admitted he mostly liked them.

"Fairies began when the first baby laughed," Peter explained. "The laugh broke into thousands of pieces and each became a fairy. Every boy and girl should have one," he added, "but they don't believe in fairies." He turned quite serious. "Did you know that each time a child says, 'I don't believe in fairies,' a fairy dies?"

Suddenly Peter remembered Tinker Bell who had remained very quiet. "Tink?" he called.

Wendy was thrilled to hear there was a fairy in her nursery but Peter laughed. "Listen," he said gleefully, "I believe I closed her in the drawer."

The sound of tinkling bells came from the dresser. Peter opened the drawer and

Tinker Bell, as angry as a hornet, flew out. She landed on the cuckoo clock.

"Oh!" cried Wendy with delight. "She is lovely! I wish she were my fairy."

Tinker Bell frowned and spoke rapidly to Peter in the tinkling bell sound that is fairy language.

"What did she say?" Wendy asked.

"She is not very polite," Peter replied. "She says you are a big, ugly girl and that she is my fairy. Of course, she can't be mine, because I am a boy and she is a girl."

On hearing that, Tinker Bell flew angrily out of the room.

Wendy wanted to know more about Peter. When he said he lived in Neverland with the lost boys, she was excited. "It must be such fun," she said.

"But we are lonely," Peter said. "There are no girls, you see. Only boys who have fallen out of their carriages are sent to Neverland. Girls are much too clever for that."

"No girls?" Wendy said. "John would

like that. He really despises girls."

On hearing that, Peter kicked John soundly out of bed. That upset Wendy.

"You may be captain in Neverland," she said, "but you are not captain here."

She softened her tone for she knew Peter did not mean to hurt John, who didn't even wake up.

"Since you meant to be kind, you may give me a kiss, I mean, a thimble," she said, remembering that Peter thought a kiss was a thimble.

The moment she leaned forward for the kiss, Tinker Bell flew into the room in a rage. She tugged Wendy's hair soundly.

"Ouch!" Wendy said. "Why did she do that?" She didn't realize that Tinker Bell was jealous.

Peter walked to the window. "It's time for me to go," he said.

Wendy was very disappointed. She was more disappointed when Peter told her the real reason he had come to the nursery window the first time.

"It was to hear the wonderful stories

your mother tells you," Peter said. "Now I must go back to Neverland to tell the boys the story she told about the prince."

"Oh, don't go," Wendy begged. "I know lots of stories."

A selfish look crossed Peter's face. He grabbed Wendy by the arm and tugged her toward the window. "Come with me and tell the other boys your stories," he said.

Wendy held back. "I can't," she said. "I

must think of my mother. And besides, I can't fly."

"I'll teach you," Peter exclaimed. "You could tell us stories and tuck us in at night." Then he smiled in a cunning way. "Oh, we would respect you so," he added. "You could sew our clothes and make pockets for us. We have none, you see. And you could see a mermaid."

"Oh!" Wendy exclaimed with delight. "Can you teach John and Michael to fly, too?"

"If you like," he said with a shrug.

Wendy shook the boys awake. "Wake up," she cried. "Peter Pan is going to teach us to fly!"

Peter took to the air as the Darling children watched with awe. It looked very easy.

"Let me try," John shouted. He leaped into the air but fell down at once.

Peter had not told the children one must have fairy dust blown on them first. He liked to tease that way. He quickly blew some fairy dust onto each child.

"Now wriggle your shoulders like this," Peter said with a wriggle of his shoulders, "and let go!"

The children did as Peter said and immediately rose into the air.

"Look at me," each shouted. "Look at me!"

"We shall go with you," Wendy called.

"There will be mermaids," Peter said, "and pirates!"

"Pirates!" John exclaimed. "Then what are we waiting for?"

The children and Peter swirled around the room like birds, though the children weren't quite as graceful as that.

Nana heard the commotion. She tugged at her chain until it pulled loose. She ran straight to the house where Mr. and Mrs. Darling were attending their party.

"Something has happened at home," Mrs. Darling exclaimed as Nana bounded into the room.

She and Mr. Darling rushed home with Nana at their heels. They ran into the house and raced up the stairs.

The children laughed aloud as they soared around the room. Suddenly, the bedroom window blew open. A tiny voice from a distant star caught Peter's ear. "Beware," the voice said. Peter knew there wasn't a moment to lose. He flew into the

night sky. "Come with me," he shouted, and John and Michael and Wendy flew out the window to join him.

At that moment Mr. Darling threw open the nursery door, but the room was as empty as a bird cage after all the birds have flown away.

Chapter

The
Flight

Peter told Wendy that the way to Neverland was, "second to the right and straight on 'til morning." It wasn't quite that easy. The children followed Peter in his flight, but Peter seemed only to follow his nose and not a map. But they didn't mind. Flying was such fun it made no difference if they were going somewhere or not.

They circled in the air like soaring birds, swooping around church spires and racing with the clouds. They lost all track of time and soon they were over the sea. When they were hungry, Peter would snatch a bit of food from a passing bird for them. When they were sleepy they would fall straight toward the sea, only to be saved at the last minute by Peter who treated the whole thing as a game. He loved to show off by sleeping on his back or by teasing sharks in the water below.

"Tell him to stop showing off," John said jealously.

"We must be nice to him," Wendy answered. "If he left us, where would we be?"

"We could go home," Michael said.

Wendy flew alongside her little brother. "But we don't know the way," she said. "We must be polite to him."

Peter had flown off for a moment and the children felt quite lonely. They were sure he had forgotten them.

"He forgets things he did only moments ago," Wendy said. "He might forget us, too."

So they continued to happily fly across the sea, though when Peter returned they were much happier.

The sun was high in the sky and the

sea below was calm when Peter pulled alongside the children. "There it is," he said. "Neverland."

Wendy, John, and Michael stretched their eyes as far as they could see. "Where?" they shouted. They stood on their tiptoes for a better look.

And suddenly they saw it, all at once. They knew in an instant it was Neverland.

"There's the lagoon," Wendy said as she pointed to the island in the sea.

"And there's your cave, Michael," John said with glee.

"I see smoke from an Indian camp!" Michael said. "It's just across the Mysterious River."

In the children's dreams, Neverland was make-believe. Now it was real. Peter was annoyed that the children already knew so much about Neverland. He wanted to be their leader. He sent Tinker Bell on ahead to scout the island.

It was growing dark as the children and Peter swooped low over the island. Wendy, John, and Michael stayed close to Peter.

Peter studied the island closely. "Would you like an adventure now?" he asked, "or would you rather have tea first?"

"Tea first," Wendy said quickly. Michael agreed, but John was more interested in adventure.

"What kind of adventure?" he asked cautiously.

"There's a pirate asleep in the plains just below us," Peter said. "If you like, we can go down and fight him."

John looked for the pirate. "I don't see him," he said.

"Well, I do," Peter answered sharply.

"What if he wakes up?" John asked nervously.

"You don't think I would attack him while he's sleeping," he said indignantly. "I would wake him first."

Now John was unsure if he wanted to attack or have tea first. "How many pirates are there?" he asked.

"More than I can count," Peter replied. "Their leader is Captain Hook."

John gulped aloud and Michael began to cry. They already knew of Captain Hook's fierce reputation.

"He's big," Peter said quickly, "but not as big as he was. I cut off a bit."

"You did?" John asked.

"His right hand," Peter replied. "Now he has an iron hook for a hand that is quite like a claw."

"A claw?" John gulped again.

"But he can still fight," Peter said, "so you must promise that if we meet him in a fight, you must leave him to me."

"I promise," John said.

It grew darker. Then Tinker Bell returned and the children could see one another in her glow. They felt less afraid. Tink whirled around them like a moth around a candle, though she was the light.

Peter didn't like Tink's lighting up everything just then. "Tink says the pirates spotted us," he said. "They saw her light and got out their cannon, Long Tom."

"Then tell her to go away," the children cried.

"No," Peter said. "She thinks we're lost and she's afraid."

"Then tell her to turn off her light," Wendy begged.

"Fairies can't turn off their lights,"

Peter said. "The lights only go off when they're asleep, and they only sleep when they are tired." He glanced at the children. "If one of us had a pocket we could carry her in it," he said. He thought for a moment. "I have it, John can carry her in his hat."

Tink agreed to hide in the hat, though not if Wendy carried it. She jumped in and John put it on his head. Immediately the children were surrounded by darkness. They flew on in silence, though many noises reached them from the island below.

Suddenly the air was rocked by a powerful roar as the pirates fired Long Tom! There was no longer any doubt that the island was real.

Peter was tossed high into the air and

out of sight by a rush of wind. Wendy and Tinker Bell, who was still in John's hat, were blown in another direction. John and Michael floated alone in the darkness.

"Are you shot?" John whispered to his brother.

"I don't know," Michael whispered back.

Luckily, nobody was hit by the cannonball.

Tinker Bell popped out of John's hat to find herself alone with Wendy. This was a perfect time for her to get rid of Wendy, for Tink was very jealous of her. She flitted back and forth in front of Wendy, filling the air with the tinkling sound of her voice. Wendy couldn't understand her, of course, but thought it meant, "Follow me."

Wendy didn't know what to do. She called for John and Michael and Peter, but nobody answered. Since Wendy didn't know that Tink didn't like her, she trusted the tiny fairy and followed. She didn't know she was flying to her own doom.

Chapter

5

The Island
Come True

Neverland came back to life now that Peter was almost there. When he was gone, everybody did nothing but wait for him to return. Now, things would be back to normal. The lost boys looked for Peter, the pirates looked for the lost boys, the Indians looked for the pirates, and the beasts looked for the Indians. Each was out to get the other in a long parade that circled the island.

The six lost boys, dressed in bearskins and with their hands upon their daggers, crept through the sugarcane in single file. Tootles, a kind and trusting lad, was in the lead. Though brave, he was always

away when adventure struck. He was just the one for Tinker Bell's plan of mischief.

Next was Nibs, and then came Slightly, who dances to music he plays on a whistle. Curly, who always takes the blame for things, was fourth, followed by the twins who nobody is quite sure which is which.

The sound of a song entered the thicket as the boys vanished into the gloom. It was the pirates' dreadful song:

"Avast, belay, yo ho, heave to,
A pirating we go,
And if we're parted by a shot
We're sure to meet below!"

The pirates were a villainous group. Cecco was in the lead. Behind him was a black man with many names, and after him, tattooed Bill Jukes. There was Gentleman Starkey, Skylights, and Smee, followed by the rest. In the middle was the most villainous one of all, the sworn enemy of Peter Pan, Captain Hook.

Trailing the pirates were the Indians

carrying tomahawks and knives. In the lead was Great Big Little Panther, his belt filled with many scalps. Bringing up the rear where the danger was greatest was Tiger Lily, the proud and beautiful Indian princess. The Indians disappeared like shadows, without making a sound.

Behind the Indians came the man-eating lions and tigers and bears with their tongues hanging out. They also vanished into the gloom.

And last of all, in a parade that nobody sees all at once, was a gigantic crocodile. It was hungry, too, but the meal it had in mind was quite special.

The boys grew tired and stopped to rest not far from their underground home.

"I wish Peter would come back," Tootles said. "Maybe he can tell us more about Cinderella." Tootles believed his mother was like Cinderella. The only time the boys could talk about mothers was when Peter was away. Tootles stopped at the sound of far-off singing. It was the grim song they knew too well:

"Yo ho ho, the pirate life,
The flag o' skull and bones,
A merry hour, a hempen rope
And hey for Davy Jones."

Before the song died away, the boys vanished into their underground home faster than rabbits down their holes. The entrances were seven hollow trees known only to the boys.

Hook had searched for the underground home for many moons, but so far, had not found it. But this time, Nibs was slow in hiding.

The pirates entered the clearing just as he disappeared into the trees. Starkey spied him. He pulled out his pistol to fire, but Hook's iron claw grabbed his shoulder.

"Put away that pistol!" Hook bellowed.

"But it was one of those boys you hate," Starkey said. "I could have shot him easily."

"And bring those Indians down on us?" Hook said, looking over his shoulder. "Do you want to lose your scalp?" Hook

rubbed his chin with his good hand. "Besides," he continued, "that was only one. I want all seven." He pointed to the woods with his hook. "Now find them!"

The pirates scurried into the woods leaving only Smee and Captain Hook behind. Hook followed them with his eyes. "Most of all, I want their leader, Peter Pan," he said to Smee. "He's the one who cut off my arm." He raised his hook threateningly. "I want to shake his hand

with this," he growled, slicing the air with the shiny metal claw. He frowned. "Peter threw my arm to a passing crocodile," he said with a painful wince.

"I've often wondered about your fear of crocodiles," Smee said.

Hook glared at him. "Not crocodiles," he said. "Just the one that ate my arm. He liked it so much he's been following me ever since hoping to dine on the other." He glared at Smee. "That's why I want Peter Pan." Hook sat down on a large mushroom with a nervous laugh. "That croc would have had me by now if he hadn't accidentally swallowed a clock," he said. "Now when I hear that clock inside him ticking, I run before he can get me."

"What will happen when the clock runs down?" Smee asked.

"That's what haunts me," Hook said through lips dry with fright. Suddenly he jumped up. He put his hand on the mushroom he'd been sitting on. "This seat is hot," he said.

The two pirates studied the strange

mushroom and then pulled it out of the ground. Smoke poured from the hole where the mushroom had been.

"Odds bobs," Hook exclaimed, "a chimney!"

They dropped to their knees. Voices rose up the chimney along with the smoke. It was the lost boys speaking without fear in the safety of their underground home.

Hook glanced around. He saw the seven trees with entrance holes. His mouth curled into a sinister smile. He tapped his nose with his hook.

"Did you hear them, Smee?" he whis-

pered. "They said Peter is not home!" His smile twisted more sharply than ever. "It's time to begin my plan," he hissed. "We'll return to the ship. There I'll bake a thick cake covered with green sugar. I'll put it on the shore of the Mermaids' Lagoon. The boys will find it when they go there to swim and play with the mermaids. They'll eat the cake and then..." He stopped to savor what would happen next. "And then, they will die!"

"Because they have no mother to tell them 'tis dangerous to eat rich cake," Smee said with delight.

"Exactly!" Hook chortled. "It is a perfect plan!"

Hook leaped into the air with glee. He opened his mouth to sing, but stopped before he could utter a note. Another sound froze him in place. It was a steady, "tick, tick, tick" that grew closer with each tick.

"The crocodile!" Hook screamed just before he disappeared into the woods with a terrified Smee right behind.

The crocodile slithered through the clearing with a strange smile on its face, but did not stop. It stayed on Hook's trail no matter where it led.

The boys emerged into the open as Nibs raced toward them pursued by a pack of wolves. "Save me!" Nibs screamed as he fell to the ground.

"What can we do without Peter?" one of the boys asked.

"Do what Peter would do," shouted another. "Look at the wolves through your legs."

The boys bent over and looked through their legs at the wolf pack. In an instant the wolves turned and fled.

Nibs got to his feet. He looked at his companions with wide eyes. "I have seen a

wonderful thing," he said in a voice filled with awe. "It was a great white bird and it's coming here." He pointed into the air. "See!"

As he spoke, a figure high in the sky descended toward the group of lost boys. Soon it was directly overhead. It was Wendy, crying because she was lost. "Poor Wendy," she cried softly, "poor Wendy."

"It's a Wendy bird," Curly said. "There are such things, you know."

When Wendy was very close, the boys heard another voice. It was Tinker Bell whom they could understand quite well. The jealous little fairy called to the boys.

"Shoot the Wendy," Tinker Bell said.

"Peter wants you to shoot the Wendy."

The boys always obeyed Peter. "Quick! Get bows and arrows," one shouted. The simple boys popped down their tree holes. Tootles stayed behind because he already had his bow and arrows.

"Quick!" Tinker Bell cried. "Shoot her now!"

Tootles loaded his bow. "Peter will be so pleased," he said. He fired. Before he could blink, Wendy fluttered to the ground with the arrow in her breast.

Chapter

6

The Little House

Tootles stood over Wendy's body like a proud hunter as the other boys popped out of their tree holes. "You're too late," he said, beaming. "I shot the Wendy. Peter will be so pleased."

Tinker Bell tinkled a little laugh and flew away to hide.

The boys silently gathered around Wendy. "This isn't a bird," Slightly said. "I think it's a lady."

"A lady?" Tootles gasped.

"We have killed her," Nibs said, taking off his cap. The others did the same.

"I think I understand," Curly said. "Peter was bringing a lady to take care of us."

Tootles backed away. "I did it," he said. "I used to dream a pretty mother would come to me, but now when she did, I shot her."

"Don't go," the others called.

"I have to," Tootles said. "I'm afraid of what Peter will say."

At that very moment Peter's call rang through the woods.

"It's Peter!" the boys cried out. They formed a circle around Wendy's body. "We must hide her," they whispered. Before they could move, Peter dropped in front of them.

"Greetings, boys!" he exclaimed.

The boys saluted mechanically, but said nothing.

"Well, I'm back," Peter said. "Why aren't you cheering?"

The boys opened their mouths but no sound came out.

"Never mind," Peter said excitedly. "I have great news. I have brought back a mother for you at last! Have you seen her? She was flying this way."

Tootles dropped to his knees. "She is here, Peter," he said sadly. He motioned to the boys to back away.

Peter stared at Wendy's body. He didn't know what to do.

"She is dead," Tootles said.

Peter took the arrow from Wendy's breast. "Whose arrow is this?" he demanded sternly.

"Mine, Peter," said Tootles.

Peter raised the arrow like a dagger. Tootles didn't flinch. He opened his shirt. "Strike me, Peter," he said.

Peter's arm would not move. "I can't strike," he said. "Something is holding me back."

While the other boys stared at Peter, Nibs glanced at Wendy. "She moved!" he cried. "The Wendy lady moved!"

Wendy had raised her arm. Nibs dropped to her side and listened. "She said, 'poor Tootles,'" he exclaimed.

"She's *alive*!" Peter shouted. He kneeled at Wendy's side. He spied the button he had given her. It was on a chain around her neck. The button was against her breast. He held up the arrow. "The arrow struck the button," he said. "It saved her life."

The tinkle of a tiny bell echoed through the woods.

"It's Tink," Curly said. "She's unhappy because Wendy is alive."

The boys told Peter what Tink had done. Peter was angrier than they had ever seen. "I am not your friend anymore," Peter called to Tinker Bell. "Be gone from me forever."

Tinker Bell flew to Peter and circled his shoulder. She pleaded not to be sent away. When Peter saw Wendy raise her arm, he changed his mind. "Well, not forever," he said to Tink with a scowl. "But for one whole week!" Then he turned his attention back to Wendy.

"What should we do with her?" one boy asked.

"Let's carry her into our house," Curly suggested.

"She is too delicate," Peter said. "We must not touch her."

The others agreed.

"But if she lies here she will die," Tootles said.

"I have an idea," Peter said. "We'll build a house around her."

The boys immediately set to work. In no time they were as busy as tailors before a wedding gathering wood and furniture and bedding.

Just then John and Michael appeared. They were exhausted and almost fell asleep standing up.

They were relieved to find Peter, even though he was too busy with Wendy's house to talk to them.

"Is Wendy sleeping?" John asked.

"Yes," Peter said sharply. "We are her servants. Now help us build her a house."

The boys protested because Wendy was a girl, but they soon gave in.

Peter thought of everything. "Fetch a doctor," he told Slightly.

Slightly walked away scratching his head, but soon returned with John's hat on his head and a solemn look on his face.

"Are you the doctor?" Peter asked.

"Yes," Slightly said. He knew it was make-believe even though Peter didn't. When the boys disagreed, Peter rapped their knuckles.

Slightly kneeled at Wendy's side. He put a make-believe thermometer in her mouth and then pretended to look at it after he removed it.

"How is she?" Peter asked anxiously.

"This has cured her," Slightly said.

"I'm glad," Peter cried.

"I will make another visit this evening," Slightly said. "In the meantime, give her a cup of beef tea." He took off John's hat when Peter wasn't looking. He was relieved not to pretend any longer.

In the meantime, the other boys had been busy. Everything was ready to build Wendy's house. "I wish we knew what kind of house she likes best," a boy said.

Hearing that, Wendy began to sing:

"I wish I had a pretty house,
  The littlest ever seen,
With funny little red walls
  And roof of mossy green."

The boys were delighted for that is exactly what they were building. The branches they gathered were covered with red sap and they had lots of moss for a roof. Soon the house was finished. It was quite beautiful, with Wendy resting comfortably inside.

Peter walked around the house, ordering finishing touches. "There's no door knocker," he said.

Tootles hung the sole of his shoe on the door.

"There's no chimney," Peter said. He punched the top out of John's hat and put it on the roof. Smoke immediately rose through it.

There was nothing left to do but knock on the door. The boys straightened themselves as Peter politely knocked. Tink sneered at them from a perch on a tree branch.

The door opened and Wendy stepped out. "Where am I?" she asked.

The boys whipped off their hats. "You are in the house we have built for you," Slightly said. "We hope you are pleased."

"It is a lovely, darling house," Wendy said.

"We are your children," the twins exclaimed.

With that all the boys fell to their knees. "Oh, Wendy lady, be our mother," they pleaded.

"Should I?" Wendy asked, beaming. "I am only a little girl."

"That doesn't matter," Peter said. "What we need is a nice motherly person."

"Oh, dear," Wendy said, "that is just what I believe I am."

"You are," the boys cried, "we knew it at once."

"Very well," Wendy said, "then I shall do my best." She looked at the boys gathered around her. "Now come inside at once. Your feet are damp so I shall have to put you to bed. But first I will finish the story of Cinderella."

The boys crowded into the tiny house with glee. Soon they were all tucked in bed and fast asleep. Wendy slept too, but Peter stayed outside with his sword drawn to protect the little house against pirates and wolves.

That was the first of many joyous evenings the lost boys spent with Wendy.

Chapter

7

The Mermaid's Lagoon

The next day, Peter measured hollow trees for Wendy, John, and Michael. They would need their own tree to enter and leave the underground home. Soon they were able to go up and down like buckets in a well.

The underground home was a marvelous place. It was one giant room. During the day the floor was anything you wanted to make it. The lost boys and Michael and John used it for play. There were mushrooms to sit on and a crackling fire, and if you wanted, you could dig a hole in the floor and go fishing. Wendy was much too busy, of course, because

she was the mother and did not have time for such things. She had to cook and clean, and at night she mended everyone's socks.

There was just one bed for the boys who slept side by side like sardines in a can. Michael slept in a hanging basket because he was the baby. Tinker Bell lived in a little room of her own that she closed at night with a curtain.

As time passed, Wendy and the boys thought less and less about their mother and father. Sometimes Michael believed Wendy was his real mother. Wendy wasn't too concerned because she was sure their parents had left a window open so she and John and Michael could fly home when the time came.

Adventure was what Neverland was all about. It had Indians and lions and tigers and bears and pirates and mermaids and much more. The difficulty was which adventure to choose.

The adventure that won took place in the Mermaid's Lagoon.

The lagoon is a lovely place of many colors where mermaids sing and play and bask on a rock in the sun. The children spent many long summer days on this lagoon, swimming and floating and playing with the mermaids. Wendy enjoyed sitting on a rock watching them as she stitched to pass the time. Sometimes the mermaids deliberately splashed water on her because they didn't really like her very much. They treated the boys the same way, though they got along well with Peter.

On sunny days after a rain, dozens of mermaids came to the surface of the lagoon to play with their bubbles. They hit them back and forth with their tails, trying to keep them in the rainbow until they burst. If the children tried to join them, the mermaids quickly disappeared beneath the water.

One sunny day the boys were dozing on Marooners' Rock. Wendy stitched as she watched over them like a mother. Suddenly, a strange shadow came over the lagoon. The air turned from warm to cold. The lagoon was no longer a friendly place, but instead was filled with danger. Wendy knew the story of Marooners' Rock. It was named by evil captains who abandoned sailors there. They would drown when the rising tide covered them. Wendy shivered. She thought to waken the children, but thought again and let them sleep. She did not want to interrupt their nap.

The sound of muffled rowing reached her ears. Peter heard it too and woke up as fast as a sleeping dog that smells danger. He put his hand to his ear and listened. "Pirates!" he cried. The sleeping boys woke with a start. "Dive!" Peter shouted.

Wendy and the boys obeyed at once. They tumbled into the water like fish poured from a barrel. In a moment Marooners' Rock was as bare as a stone in the midst of a calm green sea.

The pirates' dinghy approached the rock with Smee and Starkey pulling its oars. In back was the Indian princess, Tiger Lily. She was bound hand and foot. Though she knew her fate, her face was calm. She would be left on the rock to perish. She had been captured aboard Hook's pirate ship with a knife in her

mouth. Now she would die a death unfit for the daughter of an Indian chief.

Smee and Starkey did not see the rock in the gloom until the small boat crashed headlong into it. It took less than a minute to put their captive on the barren rock because her pride did not let her resist.

Nearby, but out of sight, Peter and Wendy watched in horror, their heads bobbing silently in the water. Wendy began to cry because she had never seen a tragedy. Peter was angry because there were two pirates against one princess. He decided to save Tiger Lily. It would be too easy to wait for the pirates to leave. He had another plan.

"Ahoy there, you lubbers," he called, imitating Captain Hook's gruff voice.

"It's our captain," Smee said with surprise.

"He is swimming to meet us," Starkey said.

"We're putting Tiger Lily on the rock," Smee cried out.

"Set her free," Peter shouted, still using the pirate captain's voice. "Cut her bonds at once."

The pirates shuddered. They dared not disobey. They knew the punishment they would get if they did.

"Aye, aye, Cap'n," Smee said, quickly cutting Tiger Lily's bonds. She slipped straight into the water like an eel.

Wendy was delighted with Peter's cleverness. Before she could say a word, Hook's voice boomed again over the water. But this time it was not Peter. It was Hook himself. He was swimming toward the pirates' dinghy. As he climbed aboard, the glow of the pirate's lantern lit his face. Wendy shuddered at the sight of his evil face.

Hook seated himself at the back of the tiny craft with a heavy sigh.

"Is something wrong, Captain?" Smee asked.

"The game is up," Hook groaned. "The lost boys have found a mother."

The pirates groaned, too. "Oh, evil day," Starkey moaned.

Wendy was filled with pride. She knew the pirates meant her.

"What's a mother?" Smee asked.

"He doesn't know!" Wendy gasped. At once she knew that Smee would be her favorite pirate, if ever there could be such a thing. Peter quickly pulled her under the water before she could say more.

"What was that?" Hook bellowed. He held the lantern to light the dark waters around the boat. The dim beam caught a strange sight.

A Never bird floated by sitting on its nest.

"That is a mother!" Hook exclaimed. "You see, its nest fell into the water, but she would not think to abandon her eggs." There was an odd catch in Hook's voice, as if some memory of his own struggled to reach the surface. He brushed it away with a pass of his iron hook.

Smee gazed at the drifting bird on her nest as it passed by. "I have an idea, Captain," he said eagerly. "We can kidnap the boys' mother and make her our mother!"

"A splendid idea!" Hook replied. He began to think. He rubbed his long chin with his hook. "We will seize the children and carry them to our boat. I will make the boys walk the plank, and Wendy shall be our mother!"

Wendy had bobbed to the surface. When she heard Hook's evil plan, she gasped, "Never!"

Luckily, the pirates did not see or hear her.

The pirates swore to carry out Hook's dreadful plan. Then, as if remembering something, he looked around the boat. "Where is Tiger Lily?" he roared.

"We let her go, Captain," Smee said. "It was your orders."

"Let her go?" Hook cried. "I gave no such order," he said with a shiver in his voice. He looked into the gloomy lagoon. "There are spirits that haunt this place," he whispered.

At the word "spirits," Smee and

Starkey wrapped their arms around one another in fear.

Hook put his good hand to his mouth. "I know you are there, spirits," he said. "Do you hear me?"

Peter could not pass up such a good prank. "I hear you," he said in a ghostly voice.

"Who are you?" Hook called out.

"I am Captain Hook, the captain of the Jolly Roger," Peter said.

Hook shook his head in disbelief. "But I am Captain Hook," he said.

"No," Peter said with a grin. "I am Hook and you are a codfish."

Smee and Starkey glanced at one another. Could it be they were commanded by a codfish, they wondered.

Hook worried that he would lose his authority over his men. He shouted into the darkness again. "Do you have another name?" he asked, hoping to trick the strange voice into revealing his identity.

"Yes," Peter said. "But you must guess it."

The pirates put their heads together but came up with nothing.

"We give up," Hook shouted.

"I am Peter Pan!" Peter shouted gleefully.

"Now we have him!" Hook said, once more in full command of his men. "After him, men," he ordered. The pirates drew their swords.

Peter cupped his hands to his mouth. "Come fight them, boys!" he called. And from all over the lagoon came the voices of the boys, each saying, "Aye, aye!"

The pirates and boys met in a fierce battle. John was in the midst of it brandishing a cutlass he tore from a pirate's grasp.

The battle was short. Hook held off the circle of attacking boys with his glistening iron hook. They backed away, fearing for their lives.

But Peter was not afraid to meet him. He climbed atop the rock as Hook joined him from the opposite side. Peter snatched a knife from Hook's belt. He was ready to use it when he saw that he was

higher on the rock than Hook. Since that made an unfair fight, Peter put out his hand to help Hook to the top. At that moment Hook struck. He clawed Peter twice with his hook. Peter fell, stunned by the blows but more by Hook's dishonesty.

Hook leaped into the water with the other pirates. They swam for their lives to their ship. Right behind them was the crocodile gnashing his silvery sharp teeth.

The boys looked everywhere for Peter and Wendy but both had vanished. They

got into the pirates' dinghy and rowed toward home. Their shouts of "Peter! Wendy!" went unanswered, except for the mocking laughter of the mermaids. The boys weren't too worried. They were sure Peter and Wendy were swimming or flying home. They hurried so they wouldn't be late for bed.

Soon after the dinghy was gone, two feeble cries drifted over the lagoon. "Help! Help!" Peter and Wendy lay on top of the rock. Peter was wounded and Wendy was tired and weak. A mermaid tried to pull Wendy into the water, but Peter pulled her back to safety.

"We have to get off the rock," Peter said. "The tide is rising. Soon we will be covered."

"I am too tired to swim or to fly," Wendy said weakly.

"And I don't have strength to carry both of us," Peter moaned.

"Then we will drown," Wendy said.

They put their hands over their eyes to shut out the horrible thought.

Something touched Peter's cheek. He opened his eyes. A kite hovered over the rock. Its long tail had brushed Peter's face. "Michael's kite!" Peter exclaimed. "He lost it the other day, but here it is!" He pulled the kite toward him. "We shall use it to carry us home."

Wendy shook her head sadly. "It can't carry two," she said. "Michael and Curly already tried."

"Then it will take you to safety," Peter said. He tied Wendy to the kite and pushed her off the rock. She was pulled into the air and was soon out of sight.

Peter was alone. The rising water tapped at his toes, ready to claim him. Far off, the mermaids sang their doleful song at the moon. Peter stood. He was afraid. Then a faint smile crossed his lips. "It will be an awfully big adventure to die," he said.

Chapter

The
Happy Home

Peter was quite alone. The mermaids had all gone to their beds beneath the sea. The only sound was the steady slurp of water rising against the rock.

Then a glimmer of something floating on the water caught Peter's eye. It looked like a bit of paper, but a closer look revealed it was the Never bird on her drifting nest.

The bird was struggling to reach Peter. She flapped her wings in the water like oars. She was nearly exhausted by the effort. It was her intention to give Peter her nest as a raft, but of course she could not tell him that. And, of course, he could not ask what her intentions were. Neither spoke the other's language.

The Never bird cackled at Peter in bird language and Peter called back in his. They grew angry because each thought the other was not really trying to understand. "Why don't you do as I tell you?" the Never bird said. And Peter replied, "What are you quacking about?" It was hopeless.

The Never bird had an idea. She decided to show Peter what she wanted. She flapped her wings and rose into the air, abandoning her nest and its cargo of precious eggs.

At once Peter understood the bird was giving up her nest so he could have a raft. But the eggs were a problem. He could not simply throw them out. Luckily, Starkey's hat hung on a post atop the rock. The post had been put there years before to mark a pirate treasure. Peter placed the big eggs in the hat and set it on the water. It floated as well as a boat.

The bird was delighted. She fluttered to the hat and sat on the eggs while Peter paddled the nest safely to shore.

In no time at all Peter was in the home under the ground. Wendy was already there. The kite had carried her straight home. The boys were thrilled to see Peter and Wendy, but they were more excited to stay up past their bedtime. Wendy would have none of that. "To bed, to bed," she said firmly. It was a voice the boys simply had to obey.

When the Indians learned that Peter had saved Tiger Lily, they became his devoted friends. They called him Chief and swore to do anything for him. The

Indian braves stood watch over the underground home to protect Peter and the others from a pirate attack. Everyone knew the pirates would attack, but they did not know when.

Peter liked being admired by the Indians and let their praise go to his head. "Your Chief is glad to see such brave warriors protecting his wigwam," he would say. On the other hand, the Indians were not so respectful to the boys. That was fine by Peter who thought that was as it should be.

Wendy secretly sympathized with the boys, but she said nothing because she did not want to upset Peter, who everyone pretended was their father. "Father knows best," she said, though she did not always believe it.

One night Peter left the underground home to get the time. The only clock on the island was inside the crocodile, so all he had to do was find the creature and wait for the chime. The Indians were at their posts above the house, while inside, the children were eating supper. It was make-believe, of course, like the rest of the adventure.

The boys broke into a squabble and Wendy had to silence them with a sharp, "Silence!"

When Peter came home he found them full of complaints. John had wanted to sit in Peter's chair; the twins complained of John; Tootles wanted to pretend he was the father, or if not, to be the baby, and Michael would not let him; Slightly coughed at the table and Curly ate both butter and honey. And on it went.

"And we want you to dance," the twins said. At first Peter refused, but since he was the best dancer, he finally gave in. Soon they were all dancing. What nobody knew was, this happy time was their last hour on the island.

The dance soon turned into an uproarious pillow fight atop the bed. But even that ended, because it was soon time for bed. The children quieted down as Wendy prepared to tell her good-night story.

Usually Peter put his hands over his ears and left the room when Wendy told her story, but tonight, he stayed on his stool to listen.

"Once upon a time there was a gentleman and a lady," Wendy began. But before she could continue, the boys interrupted.

"*Was* a lady?" cried one of the twins. "Do you mean she is dead?"

"I wish the gentleman was a white rat," Nibs said.

"Be quiet," Wendy scolded. "No, the lady is not dead," she said, getting back to her story.

"I'm glad," Tootles said.

"Sssh!" Peter hushed. "A little less noise!"

"The gentleman's name was Mr. Darling," Wendy said. "The lady's name was Mrs. Darling."

"I knew them once," John said, to annoy the others.

"I think I knew them, too," Michael said, though he was not so sure.

Wendy ignored the interruptions. "The lady and gentleman were married," she said. "And they had three descendants."

"Descendants only means children," John said.

Wendy touched her finger to her lips before continuing. "The three children had a faithful nurse called Nana," she said. "But one night, Mr. Darling chained her in the yard because he was angry with her." She glanced at the boys and Peter who listened wide-eyed. "That night the children flew away to Neverland where the lost children are," Wendy went on. "And they are there still."

"Was one of the lost children called Tootles?" Tootles asked excitedly. Wendy nodded. "Hooray!" Tootles crowed. "I am in a story."

"Ssh!" Wendy hushed. "Just think of those unhappy parents with all of their children flown away."

Everyone moaned, though they really weren't much interested in unhappy parents at all.

"How can this story have a happy ending?" a twin asked.

"If you knew how much a mother loves her children, you would know," Wendy said. Peter didn't like this part of the story, but Wendy continued to tell the rest. "The oldest child knew the mother would leave the window open," she said. "That way the children could return whenever they wanted."

"Did they go back?" Tootles asked.

Wendy tapped the side of her nose. "We have to look into the future to see," she said with her eyes looking off. "Many years later an elegant woman steps off the train. It is, my goodness, it is Wendy!" she

said with a smile. "And with her are two handsome gentlemen. Why, it is John and Michael!"

"Oh!" John and Michael gasped to hear they were in the story.

"The three are in front of a house," Wendy said, still telling the story. "Now Wendy points to the open window. 'There is our reward for trusting our mother's love,' she says." Wendy turned to the boys. "And that is the happy ending!"

"Ohhh! I am ill," Peter groaned.

Wendy ran to him at once. "Where does it hurt?" she asked.

He put his hand over his heart. "Here,"

he said. But he wasn't really ill, of course. It was the story that hurt him. "You are wrong about mothers, Wendy," he said. "I used to think my mother would keep a window open for me, too, but when I went back the window was barred. She had forgotten all about me."

The idea of being forgotten frightened John and Michael. "Let's go home, Wendy," they cried.

Wendy gathered them in her arms. "Yes," she said. "Tonight!"

"Not tonight!" the lost boys cried in bewilderment.

"We'll leave at once," Wendy said. The

thought had suddenly occurred to her that her mother's heart was half-broken with her children gone. "Peter," she said quickly, "will you make the necessary arrangements?"

"If you wish," Peter said calmly, trying to keep his real feelings hidden. He hurried up the hollow tree to tell the Indians what to do. When he returned to the home under the ground, the lost boys had rebelled.

"It will be worse for us than before she came," they shouted, frightened by the thought of losing Wendy. "We shall keep her prisoner!"

But Tootles would have none of it. "Don't touch her!" he cried. The other boys withdrew.

Just then Peter stepped into the room. "We won't keep you against your will," he said. "The Indians will guide you through the woods and Tinker Bell will lead you across the sea."

Tinker Bell was delighted Wendy would be leaving, but she was not eager to be her guide. Peter gave her a warning stare and she quickly changed her mind.

John and Michael prepared for the journey as the lost boys watched dejectedly.

Wendy's heart melted at the sight of the sad lost boys. "You can come with us," she said. "I am sure my father and mother will adopt you."

"Can we go, Peter?" the boys shouted excitedly.

Peter nodded that they could, though his heart was not in it. The boys rushed out to get their things.

"And you'll come, too," Wendy said to Peter.

"No!" Peter said calmly. "I am not going."

"But it's to find your mother," Wendy said.

"No," Peter said. "I don't need a mother. And besides, I want to stay a little boy and have fun."

The lost boys returned, each with a bundle on the end of a stick. When they

heard Peter wasn't coming, they were stunned.

But that was that, so Wendy gathered everyone for the journey. "Remember to change your flannels and take your medicine," she said to Peter.

"Yes, I will," Peter said as if he were hiding his real feelings. He turned to Tinker Bell. "Lead the way for them," he said.

Tink immediately darted up the nearest hollow tree. But nobody followed, because at that very moment the room filled with the sound of clanking steel and rough voices.

The pirates had attacked!

Chapter

The Children
are Carried Off

The attack came as a complete surprise. The pirates had sneaked quietly through the forest until they were close to the home beneath the ground. There they waited for dawn. Hook had learned this tactic from the Indians. The Indians guarding the secret lair knew the pirates were on the island, of course, but they did not expect an attack before dawn. They sat quietly with blankets wrapped around them, unaware that Hook and his evil band were so near.

The pirates swooped into the Indian camp just before daylight. An alert scout uttered a coyote cry as a warning, but it

was too late. When the stunned Indians saw the pirates, they leaped to their feet. A dozen braves circled Tiger Lily to protect her. Others ran to meet the cutlass-wielding buccaneers. The air filled with war cries, the ring of cold steel against iron tomahawks and the shouts of fallen men.

It was a gruesome battle in which many perished on both sides, but the pirates did not let up their attack. Soon the small circle of Indians protecting Tiger Lily was all that remained of the tribe. Fighting for their lives, the Indians cut their way through the ring of pirates and escaped.

Hook was elated, but he was not satisfied. It was Peter Pan he was after. The pirate despised Peter. True, Peter had thrown Hook's arm to the crocodile, which was reason enough to dislike someone, but Hook's hatred went beyond that. It wasn't Peter's good looks or courage that drove Hook crazy. It was Peter's utter cockiness. Hook vowed to smash the bothersome youth like a mosquito.

Hook studied the hollow trees leading to the underground home. The openings were too narrow for fat pirates. He looked over his motley band for someone who could wriggle his way into the cavern below.

In the meantime, the children had heard the sounds of battle over their heads. They listened, frozen with fear, to the whoops of men and the clang of steel. Now it was silent. Wendy, John, Michael, Peter, and the lost boys stared at one another. The same question was on everyone's lips: "Which side won?"

Peter gazed upward, with a hand cupped to his ear. "If the Indians have won, they will beat their tom-tom as a sign of victory," he said.

The others cupped their ears to listen.

A pirate near a hollow tree heard what Peter said and reported it to Hook. Hook grinned a devilish smile. He turned to Smee. "Beat the drum," he said.

Smee chuckled at his captain's devious plan. He beat the drum in the Indian manner.

"Listen!" Peter exclaimed when he heard the victory tom-tom. "The Indians have won!"

"We can leave after all," Wendy said.

The children said good-bye to Peter and made ready to hurry up the hollow trees for their journey home.

But the pirates had other plans. They smirked and rubbed their hands as they waited for the children to pop out of the hollow trees.

Curly was the first one out. He fell into

the hands of a pirate who quickly passed him on to another. One by one the children were captured as they stepped out of the openings in the hollow trees. Wendy was last.

Hook removed his hat and bowed graciously when he saw Wendy. He personally escorted her to where the boys were being tightly bound with stout ropes so they could not escape. Wendy was surprised by Hook's unusual politeness and did not cry out even when she too, was tied.

Hook watched with pleasure as his men tied up the children. As Slightly was being tied, the sinister captain noticed something about the boy that nobody else had seen. Slightly was swollen round from his habit of drinking too much water. This could mean only one thing. The opening in Slightly's hollow tree had to be large enough for a man to slip through. If so, Hook could let himself into the home under the ground.

As the pirates carried the children off

to their ship, Hook tiptoed to Slightly's hollow tree and slithered down the hole like a snake. He stood behind the door at the bottom and listened. The cavernous room was silent. Hook peered through a crack in the door. He wiped his smirking lips with the back of his hand. Across the room, lying sound asleep on his bed was Peter, his sworn enemy. Peter's medicine bottle was on a table next to the bed. The medicine had not been touched. Hook knew at once how he would get rid of Peter forever.

Hook carried a bottle of powerful poi-

son with him at all times. It was a vile, yellow substance he had concocted himself. He slipped the bottle from his sash and poured five potent drops into Peter's medicine cup. It was everything he could do to keep from shouting for joy. Hook knew that the moment Peter took his medicine, he would be done with him forever. Satisfied that the deed was done, Hook slipped back up the hollow tree and disappeared into the forest.

Peter was sleeping soundly when a tapping at the door awoke him. He reached for his dagger. "Who is it?" he called.

The sound of tinkling bells filled the air. Peter smiled. It was Tink. He quickly opened the door.

The tiny fairy burst into the room. Peter saw at once that she was upset. "What's the matter, Tink?" he asked.

Tinker Bell told Peter how the pirates had captured Wendy and the boys and how they were at that moment prisoners on the pirate ship.

"I'll rescue her!" Peter shouted. He hurried to get his weapons. He stopped suddenly as he passed the table with his medicine cup. "I did not take my medicine because I wanted to displease Wendy," he said. "Now I shall take it to show that I care." He lifted the cup to his lips.

"No!" Tinker Bell shrieked. She had heard Hook as he raced through the forest, boasting aloud what he had done. She knew the cup contained deadly poison. "It's poisoned!" she cried.

"Don't be silly," Peter said. He tipped the cup.

Tinker Bell darted between the cup and his lips. In an instant she drank the potion to the last drop to save Peter. She staggered backward. Already the deadly brew was working. She settled softly on Peter's shoulder.

"Oh, Tink!" Peter exclaimed. "It really was poisoned. You did it to save me." He put his hand to his face. "Why, Tink? Why did you do it?"

Tinker Bell raised herself to her feet

and gave the tip of his nose a loving bite. She flew weakly to her bed and fell upon it.

Peter poked his head into Tink's tiny room. Her light was flickering and growing faint. Once it went out, Tink would be gone forever. Peter began to cry. Large teardrops ran down his face.

Tink whispered weakly. Peter put his ear close to hear what she was saying. "I can get well again if children believe in fairies," she said softly.

Peter threw up his hands. "But there are no children here," he said. Then he thought of all the children of the world who were sleeping and dreaming of Neverland. "Don't let Tink die!" he cried out to them. "If you believe in fairies, clap your hands."

Tink sat up to listen for the children's answer. From all around the world came the faint sound of children clapping. Not all of them, of course, but enough to save Tink. Her voice grew strong. Then she popped out of bed. In seconds she was darting around the room as bright and merry as before.

"And now to rescue Wendy!" Peter shouted. He dashed to his hollow tree and in an instant popped out into the world above.

The moon was bright. Peter wanted to fly, but if he did, his shadow would trail through the trees and disturb the birds. Their chirping would alert the pirates of his coming. He would have to sneak through the forest like an Indian.

"It will be Hook or me this time," he said. He was quite excited for this, like every adventure, was great fun.

Chapter

The Pirate Ship

The pirates carried the children to Captain Hook's ship, the *Jolly Roger*, lying at anchor on Kidd's Creek. The grim craft was covered with the bloody stains of piracy and war. She was a cannibal of the sea and reeked of horror. The children were locked in the brig below.

The men leaned over the ships' low rails staring at the ink-black sea or sat on deck playing cards or dice. Smee, the pirate despised by all because he was so pathetic, sat at his sewing machine, quietly at work.

Hook stalked the deck, deep in thought. He had just rid himself of Peter forever and the children were doomed to walk the plank. But there was no joy on the captain's dark face. On the contrary, he was dejected and alone. "No little children love me!" he thought. The idea had not bothered him before, but now, as he watched Smee, it did. Children thought Smee was lovable, though Smee himself thought children feared him. Hook wanted to clout Smee with his iron claw, but stopped short. Unhappiness overwhelmed him.

Hook quickly turned his attention to

the children. "Are they chained so they can't fly away?" he bellowed.

"Aye, sir," answered a pirate.

"Then hoist them up," Hook ordered.

All but Wendy were dragged from the hold and lined up in front of Captain Hook. Hook stroked his chin. "Six of you will walk the plank tonight," he said with a hint of pleasure in his voice. "But two of you I need for cabin boys. Which of you will they be?"

"I don't think my mother would want me to be a pirate," Tootles said. Slightly said the same and so did the twins.

Hook was annoyed. "Stow the gab," he roared and then turned to John. "You look like you want to be a pirate, my hearty," he said.

The truth was, sometimes in school, John had thought about being a pirate. "I once thought to call myself Red-Handed Jack," John replied.

Hook beamed. "A good name, that," he said. "And what about you?" he asked, turning to Michael.

"What would my name be if I join?" Michael asked.

"Blackbeard Joe," Hook said.

Michael was impressed. "What do you think, John?" he asked his brother.

"Would we have to give up our citizenship?" John asked.

"You would have to swear, 'Down with the king!' " Hook demanded.

"Then I refuse," John said, banging his fist on a barrel.

"And so do I," Michael joined in.

The lost boys shouted their approval.

"Then your fate is sealed," Hook shouted. "Bring up their mother," he ordered, "and prepare the plank!"

The boys were frightened but each tried to look brave when Wendy was brought up from below.

"So, my beauty," Hook said in a voice dripping with honey, "you are here to see your children walk the plank, eh?"

"Are they to die?" Wendy asked.

"Yes!" Hook said sharply. "If you have any last words for them, speak them now."

Wendy looked into each boy's face.
"These are the last words all mothers
would say to their children." She said
firmly, "I hope you will be brave and die
like English gentlemen."

The pirates were awed. The boys stared
at one another. "We will do as our mothers' hope," they said.

"Silence!" Hook shouted. "Tie her to
the mast."

Smee tied Wendy to the mast in the
center of the foul ship. "I'll save you if you
promise to be my mother," he whispered
into her ear.

Wendy shook her head. "Never," she said scornfully.

The boys weren't watching Wendy. Their eyes were glued on the plank. Their thoughts were on the last walk they would soon take.

Hook grinned fiendishly. Suddenly the grin turned to horror. The night breeze carried with it the steady "tick-tick-tick" of the fearsome crocodile. "The crocodile is going to board my ship!" he exclaimed. The terrified captain fell to the deck and crawled as fast as he could to a dark corner. "Hide me!" Hook shouted. His men formed a tight circle around him.

The moment Hook was out of sight, the boys rushed to the rail. To their great joy and surprise, it was not the toothsome crocodile climbing the side of the ship. It was Peter!

Peter put his finger to his grinning lips to quiet the boys and then went on ticking.

Chapter

Hook or Me This Time

Peter had sneaked through the jungle unseen. Midway to Kidd's Creek he passed the crocodile that, as always, was on Hook's trail. It was not ticking because the clock had run down. Peter grinned as a clever idea occurred to him. He imitated the ticking sound. It was perfect. Even the crocodile thought it was real and began to follow Peter.

Peter swam easily across the open water to the ship. He scampered up its side, still ticking. "It will be Hook or me this time," he thought as he hoisted himself over the rail. The boys stood silently by so they would not give him away.

A pirate strolled past, gazing at the stars. Peter pushed him over the rail.

"One down," Slightly whispered, and began to keep count.

Captain Hook peered from his hiding place behind the ring of men. The ticking sound had stopped. He emerged as if he had not been scared out of his wits. His eyes glowed red and his scowl turned sinister once more. "Get these boys to Johnny Plank," he ordered, pointing to the plank hanging over the ship's side. He leaped onto the plank and began to dance along its precarious length. A devilish grin crossed his face as he sang:

"Yo ho, ho, the frisky plank
You walk along it so,
Till it goes down and you go down,
To Davy Jones below!"

Hook jumped to the deck. "But first, a bit of the whip for these prisoners," he said.

"No!" the boys shouted.

Jukes, a pirate, hurried to the cabin to fetch the dreaded cat o' nine tails.

"Peter is in the cabin," Slightly whispered to the cowering boys.

A dreadful screech burst from the dark cabin.

"What was that?" Hook cried.

"Two down," Slightly said with a grin.

Another pirate dashed into the cabin but burst out a second later. "Jukes is gone," he gasped. "There's something terrible in there."

Hook eyed his men. "Get in there and see what it is," he hissed at Cecco.

Cecco entered the cabin cautiously.

Another horrible screech split the air.

"Three," Slightly said.

The pirate captain turned to Starkey. "I believe I heard you volunteer," he said.

"No!" Starkey said defiantly. "I won't go in there."

"So it's mutiny, is it?" Hook growled.

Starkey glanced at the ring of pirates gathered around Captain Hook. None of them moved. Starkey eyed the dark cabin and then the captain's gleaming iron hook. Neither choice looked good. He spun on his heel and leaped over the rail into the sea.

"Four," Slightly whispered to the other boys.

Hook polished his claw against his coat. "If none of you will go, I'll fetch that cat myself," he said. He grabbed a flickering lantern and stepped to the cabin door.

Slightly pursed his lips, ready to count "Five," but Hook staggered out before any damage was done. "Something blew out the light," he muttered.

"Someone's aboard who doesn't

belong," a pirate said. "Maybe it's the devil."

"The ship is doomed," another cried.

Hook touched his nose with the tip of his hook. "Send the prisoners in," he said. "If they beat what's in there, or it beats them, we'll be none the worse."

The pirates shoved the boys into the cabin and slammed the door behind them. They turned away so they would not have to witness what was sure to follow.

Inside the cabin, Peter unlocked the chains binding the boys. They all found weapons and on Peter's hushed command, sneaked out the door, unseen.

Peter ran to Wendy and cut her bonds with his dagger. Now nothing prevented Peter and the children from flying to safety. But Peter's vow rang in his ears. "Hook or me this time," he had said. They would fight to the finish.

Peter wrapped Wendy's cloak around himself and put his back to the mast as Wendy hid in the darkness with the boys. Peter uttered a loud scream.

The pirates were certain the noise signalled the end of the boys. They were panic-stricken. Whatever was in the cabin would surely come for them now.

Hook sensed mutiny. He quickly turned to the mast. "It's the girl," he snarled. "A woman on a pirate ship brings bad luck. When she's gone, we'll get rid of what's in that cabin." He raised his clawed arm. "Throw her overboard," he shouted.

The pirates dashed for the cloaked figure at the mast. It was time for Peter to strike. He threw the cloak to the deck and brandished his dagger.

"Peter Pan!" Hook screamed. At once he and his men knew what it was that had lurked inside the cabin. His black heart thumped with fear, but the fight was gone out of him. "Get him!" he ordered, but his voice was weak.

"Attack, boys!" Peter shouted to the children. They burst from hiding and went

straight for the pirates. One by one the pirates fell or were tossed overboard. Slightly could scarcely keep count. The din of battle echoed over the water until, at last, only one pirate remained. The band of boys surrounded him with their gleaming swords high in the air.

"Put away your swords, boys," Peter

shouted. He jumped into the circle to face Captain Hook alone. "This one is mine," he said.

Hook glared at Peter. "Prepare to meet thy doom," he hissed. The pirate captain leaped at Peter with his hook and sword slashing the air.

Peter quickly danced out of danger. He thrust with his own sword to nip Hook's coat. Hook nimbly escaped a more serious blow. He slashed back at Peter. Again Peter parried the captain's attack. Again and again the two exchanged strikes. Again and again they avoided the worst.

A sudden thrust by Peter sent Hook's

sword flying to the deck. Disarmed, Hook was doomed. But Peter bowed graciously and allowed his evil foe to recover the fallen weapon. Hook was enraged by Peter's good manners.

"Who are you?" Captain Hook shouted, still fighting for his life.

"I'm youth and joy!" Peter exclaimed, still pursuing his faltering prey.

The two fought on, but Hook was clearly finished. In desperation, the pirate gave up the fight. He dashed into the powder warehouse and lit the fuse of a powerful cannonball. "The ship will be blown to pieces in two minutes!" Hook crowed. He desperately wanted to see Peter turn tail and flee for his life.

Peter rushed into the warehouse. He grabbed the sputtering bomb and hurled it overboard as calmly as if it were a scrap of bread for a passing gull. Once more Peter's good form got the better of Hook.

Outfought and outwitted, Hook was beaten in every way. He staggered to the rail and climbed to its top. If he could not

win, he would escape, even though it meant showing the worst form of all. With his black locks and long-tailed coat flying in the wind, Hook prepared to leap into the sea. He stared down at the dark water. A pair of eyes stared back. The crocodile snapped its powerful jaws. Hook shuddered. He turned his back to Peter.

Peter stepped forward and with a swift kick, sent Hook toppling into the sea. "Bad form," Hook jeered, as he vanished forever.

The pirates were beaten. Peter and the boys raised a victory cheer as Wendy stepped out from the shadows. "It's very late," she said, "and time for bed." Without protest, the exhausted children lay down and soon were fast asleep.

Chapter

The Return Home

The pirate ship plowed through the sea with its crew of children and its captain, Peter Pan, at the helm. With luck, they would reach the Azores by the end of June. It would be easy to fly home from there. Wendy, John, and Michael had been gone for a very long time. They were eager to return and looked forward to the surprise on their mother's face.

In the meantime, Mr. and Mrs. Darling waited. Mrs. Darling kept the nursery just as it was, although Nana's kennel was moved out. Mr. Darling felt it was his fault the children were gone, since it was he who had chained Nana in the yard that fateful night. To show his remorse, he stayed in the kennel and refused to come out.

The first ones to reach the house at Number 14 were Peter Pan and Tinker Bell. They flew to the open window. "Quick, Tink," Peter said. "Close the window and bar it. When Wendy returns, she'll think her mother does not want her back. Then she'll come back to Neverland with me."

Peter had planned this trick all along. He did not want Wendy to return home at all. He flew to another window and glanced in. "It's Mrs. Darling," he

exclaimed. The children's mother had fallen asleep at the piano. "She's pretty, but not as pretty as my mother," Peter said. Of course, Peter didn't know his own mother, even though he liked to brag that he did. "You will never see Wendy again," he whispered.

Two fresh tears sparkled on Mrs. Darling's cheeks. Peter stared at them. "She is awfully fond of Wendy," he said. "She wants the window open so the children can come back. But then Wendy won't be able to stay with me. We can't both have her." He could not take his eyes off Mrs. Darling's sad face. "Oh, all right," he gulped. He quickly opened the nursery window. "Come on, Tink, *we* don't want any silly mothers." He turned his back to the window and flew away.

Soon Wendy, John, and Michael reached the house. The window was open for them after all. They flew inside and landed gently on the floor. Each looked around as if they had forgotten it was their home.

"I think I've been here before," Michael said.

"Of course you have, silly," John replied. "There's your bed. And there's the kennel."

"Maybe Nana is inside," Michael exclaimed.

Just then a noise from the hall warned the children that someone was coming. "It's Mother!" Wendy exclaimed.

"Then you're not really our mother?" Michael asked in a sleepy voice.

Wendy shook her head. She pointed to the beds. "Quickly," she said. "Get into bed as if we've never been away."

The children jumped into their beds and pulled up the covers.

When Mrs. Darling peeked into the

room, she saw at once that all the beds were full. She was sure she was dreaming. She sat down in her chair, just as she had when they were babies.

"Mother!" Wendy cried.

"That's Wendy," Mrs. Darling said.

"Mother!" John shouted.

"That's John," Mrs. Darling said.

"Mother!" Michael crowed.

"And that's Michael," Mrs. Darling said, certain at last it was not a dream. She stretched out her arms for her children who leaped out of bed and ran to her. "George! George!" Mrs. Darling called to her husband. She wrapped her arms tightly around the children and held them

very close. There never was a lovelier sight.

Outside the window a small face stared into the cozy room. It was the little boy whose life was filled with adventure and joy. But now, looking in through the window, Peter Pan saw the one joy he would never, ever know.

The lost boys were waiting outside. Wendy quickly explained to her mother they would like to come in, too. Soon Slightly, Tootles, Curly, Nibs, and the twins were in the children's room. They

were still dressed in their pirate clothes. Each boy looked into Mrs. Darling's eyes as if to say, "May we please stay?"

Mrs. Darling agreed immediately to let the boys stay, but Mr. Darling was not so sure. After all, there were six of them and the Darlings already had three.

"If we would be too much of a handful, we will go away," the first twin said.

"We will share a bed," Nibs said.

"I will cut their hair," Wendy said.

"We'll fit in, sir," Tootles said.

Mr. Darling nodded. "Yes," he said, "you can stay."

"Hoopla!" the boys shouted, and they all danced through the house with joy.

Peter had not yet returned to Neverland. He flew by the window and Wendy opened it to let him in.

"Good-bye, Wendy," he said.

"Are you really going?" Wendy asked.

Mrs. Darling entered the room. She smiled at Peter and asked him to stay.

"Would you send me to school?" Peter asked.

"Of course," Mrs. Darling replied.

"And I would have to grow up?" Peter asked.

"Of course," Mrs. Darling replied.

"I don't want to grow up," Peter said. "I'm going back to Neverland to live with Tink in a house in the trees." He glanced at Wendy. "It will be such fun," he said, hoping she would go with him.

"May I go with Peter, Mother?" Wendy asked.

"Of course not," Mrs. Darling said.

"But he needs a mother," Wendy said.

"And so do you," Mrs. Darling answered. "But you may visit Peter once each spring to help with his spring cleaning."

Wendy agreed, though she would have preferred to go right now. She turned to Peter. "You won't forget me, will you, Peter?" she asked.

"Of course not," Peter promised. And then he flew away.

Soon the lost boys were in school. Some did well, while others had to struggle. After a time they all forgot how to fly, even Michael. They no longer believed they could.

Peter came for Wendy the next year, but she was surprised to learn he had already forgotten many of their adventures together. He didn't even remember Captain Hook or Tinker Bell because his head was filled with new adventures.

The next year, Wendy waited for Peter in vain. He did not come. Many more years passed, and Wendy was quite grown up. She didn't mind at all that she was grown. In fact, she liked it. Peter became a distant memory. The boys grew up too, and each went his own way in life, just as they should.

Wendy married and had a daughter of her own, named Jane, who was just as inquisitive as her mother. She loved to hear the stories of Peter Pan, and remembered every one. Jane lived in the same nursery Wendy did when she was little.

One night after Wendy finished telling a story, Peter Pan himself flew in the window. He had no idea so many years had passed, for he was still a boy.

Wendy felt strange because she was grown up and Peter had not changed one bit.

"Hello, Wendy," Peter said.

"Hello, Peter," Wendy replied.

Peter glanced around the room. "Where is John?" he asked. "And where is Michael?"

"They aren't here anymore," Wendy said.

"Have you forgotten that this is spring-cleaning time?" Peter asked.

"I can't go with you, Peter," Wendy said. "I've forgotten how to fly. I'm grown up now. Let me turn up the light and you'll see."

Peter was afraid for the first time in his life. "No," he said. But it was too late. The moment the light came on, he saw Wendy was a woman and not a little girl.

Peter sat on the floor and began to cry. His sobs woke Jane.

"Why are you crying, boy?" Jane asked. They were the very words Wendy first said to Peter, many years before.

Peter stood quickly and bowed very low. "My name is Peter Pan," he said.

"Yes, I know," Jane said. "I've been waiting for you." Instantly she began to fly around the room.

"She is my mother," Peter said to Wendy.

Wendy shook her head sadly. "Yes," she

said. "Nobody knows that as well as I."

Peter flew into the air. "Good-bye, Wendy," he said. Jane flew to join him and the two darted to the window.

"No!" Wendy shouted as she ran to the window.

"It's just for spring cleaning time," Jane said to her mother.

Wendy knew she could not hold them back. Peter flew out the window with Jane trailing joyfully behind.

"If only I could go with you," Wendy sighed.

When Jane grew up, she also had a daughter. When spring cleaning time came, she too flew off with Peter Pan to be his mother. And so it will be forever, as long as there are little children.

THE END

ABOUT THE AUTHOR

JAMES MATTHEW BARRIE was born in 1860 in Kirriemuir, Scotland. From a very early age, Barrie loved acting and writing plays. When he graduated from Edinburgh University, he moved to London and began a career as a drama critic and journalist.

Barrie's most famous book is *Peter Pan*, but he is the author of numerous works.

The Young Collector's
Illustrated Classics

Adventures of Robin Hood
Black Beauty
Call of the Wild
Dracula
Frankenstein
Heidi
Little Women
Moby Dick
Oliver Twist
Peter Pan
The Prince and the Pauper
The Secret Garden
Swiss Family Robinson
Treasure Island
20,000 Leagues Under the Sea
White Fang